Gossip!

Sushil Thind

Michael Terence
Publishing

First published in paperback by
Michael Terence Publishing in 2021
www.mtp.agency

ISBN 9781800941304

One

She puts on her red lipstick after the finishing touches of her makeup. Smiling in the mirror. New day. New beginning. The love of her life still in the shower, after a long night.

She looks out of the window, the sky is blue with the sun shining through. Wow, new day lots to do. Looking through her wardrobe she cannot make up her mind on what to wear. The noise of the shower stops. She was daydreaming, not realising he's behind her. She exclaims because he's just given her a fright. She jumps out of her skin then starts laughing. You just frightened the life out of me. Putting her hand on her chest she falls into his arms.

He kisses her and asks her who else was it going to be? The Neighbour?

I'm still looking for an outfit to wear cannot make up my mind.

Let me see he replies. How about we wear similar colours.

Mmm, not sure about that. She pulls out a black and red dress.

Okay cool.

Everyone is happy. Matching like his and hers or Mr and Mrs. Today is our day. No phone calls, no emails, no messages. Just us. As if that will last! Haha. They both laughed.

Seriously we sometimes have to leave work behind. That's why there are so many breakups because of lack of time for each other.

True, she replies. I'm glad we're on the same page, babe.

He calls the restaurant and makes a booking so they will be there by 8pm. Oh, here we go… the phone starts ringing, Is he going to answer?

She has her fingers crossed hoping he will keep his side of the bargain. He looks at her and ignores the phone. Then message after message. She looks at him with a frown.

Oh, just answer it or they are not going to leave you alone.

Okay, just one message. He replies quickly. It's the new guy. He is very ambitious. I've left him in charge. I told him to call and message if he struggles. He just wanted to pass some information by me before sending it off.

She gives him a thumbs up They cooked and had their lunch.

She said, you work too hard.

Well we both do.

Okay. Maybe I said that wrong; we both do.

They decided to watch a Netflix movie that they had been trying to watch for a while. Yay, at last, get the popcorn and the wine. I will have the red.

Yes, I've made sure it's the red.

I've poured the wine and the popcorn is there. Yes, yes, I'm doing the washing, I know how it goes. Haha. But you will put out the bins. Actually, we will together.

The movie is coming on quickly babe. He puts the popcorn on his lap and the wine on the table. Puts his arm around her.

They laugh at the funny parts. Just being here spending time together is so special…

The movie is nearly over; it's been nearly two hours.

Oh, my gosh! What's the time he said.

Why? What is the matter?

I've booked a table for eight o'clock.

What really? Aww, my babe, you're so sweet. Okay, I can't go like this. Oh, no.

What have I done, he laughs. You are beautiful and sexy the way you are.

Oh, come on. No way! I'm not leaving the house like this.

Okay, well hurry up.

She goes and pulls out a few dresses. Which one do you think? She holds one in her hand and is wearing another.

Aww yeh, I love you in that one.

Anyway, she rolls her eyes in despair. Men! and starts laughing.

She ends up wearing a jumpsuit. Touches-up on the makeup while he now decides to wear a different shirt. She sighs and tells him how handsome he looks in anything and nothing.

He replies, I know.

She replies, charming, and starts to laugh and gives him a hug and smiles.

They finally leave to go to the restaurant and enjoyed their meal. It was delicious.

He orders some dessert.

I will be back. She goes to touch up her lipgloss.

Don't be too long, babe.

Okay sweet.

While she is gone, he tells the waitress to place the ring he is going to give her in her dessert dish. The waitress does so and brings it over. She saw the waitress leaving.

Ooh, she looks very happy did you tip her? Is everything okay? genuinely asking.

Yes, everything is fine.

Shall I pay?

No, no, it's okay.

I wasn't sure about the dessert.

Oh, okay. Desert arrives.

So is your dessert okay? he asked.

Yes. Why? You're acting a bit weird. She looks at him. Just asking.

I always love this dessert every time we come here.

Mine's a little harder than usual.

Really. Why? Is the spoon not going through? Keep trying you're probably not digging the spoon in properly.

Oh, come on, babe. I know how to use a spoon. She smiles. Hold on there is something in here. Oh, my gosh, really? Yeh. I'm going to pull it out.

Okay.

She puts her fingers in the dessert dish and pulls it out.

It's a ring!! she screams.

He looks around and whispers, sssh…

She cleans it and puts it on her finger. I know it's a little late. The stone had to be ordered specially.

Oh my god! I love you so much, babe. I thought you were not getting me anything.

Don't be silly. You know me; a very sentimental kinda guy.

She was so happy that she reached out for her mobile to boast, of course.

That's fine, the evening is over anyway, babe!

She calls her sister and screams down the mobile… Aaaa, guess what, sis. Have you seen it? her sis replies. What? You knew about it.

The sister starts laughing. Yeh, he told me about it. What do you think?

It's beautiful.

I've got to go, the little one has only just fallen asleep.

Oops, sorry, speak tomorrow. Love you, sis.

Love you too. Good night.

She comes off the phone and has a big smile on her face. I'm never taking it off. That's the whole idea, babe.

That's a good idea, he said.

Two

In the morning, she makes some coffee once she is out of the shower and he makes their breakfast.

Getting ready to go back to run their business…

Mmm, you smell so good.

You would say that.

Why? she reacts, because you bought it for me. She smiles.

Only the best, ay? Yesterday was a good day. We needed it. It was refreshing, wasn't it?

Yeh, definitely.

Let's see how things have been at the office.

Yep, surely it's okay.

Meet you at lunchtime, if I can.

Okay, babe. See you later. They kiss and leave the house, each in their own cars.

Someone sees him walking into the office; he overhears a conversation: The boss has been with his partner for two years yesterday. We should have got him something. Shh, he's coming. He smiles as he has overheard the gossip and carries on into the office after giving everyone a smile and saying morning to all.

They continue: We can't because we're not supposed to know, remember? Mentions another. Then they all go back to their own tables and carry on working.

The neighbour is out, just taking the dog for a walk, and waves. The couple wave back, smiling. He starts a conversation: Seeing you reminds me of me when I was your age. I can see you're busy. Waves and carries on.

After work usually they would go for a run. They had recently joined a keep fit program. Not because they needed to but because they had sponsored a keep fit program. Set an example. Without a doubt, they would go for a run a few times each week.

The next day when they went to the gym, she watches him on the weights. Wow, pumping his muscles. She takes a deep breath all flustered, feeling thirsty, drinks her water and plugs in her AirPods.

Whispering to herself… calm, she carries on running the treadmill, thinking to herself what am I like? He's mine. He's mine!

There's a man who has been looking at her kind of talking to herself. He goes up to her and says. you okay, love?

She replies, oh, yeh, I'm fine thanks.

He goes one: I thought you needed some help as you looked like you were talking to yourself.

Oh, she said. Haha. I was plugged in and singing!

Oh, okay, that fine.

I'm here if you need any help.

Thank you, she replies. Her one and only looks at her and asks her if she's okay because the man went up to her.

She replies, yeh, yeh, I'm good. He was just asking if I needed a hand. He does work at the gym, after all.

Okay, he replies.

She looks at the time. They've been there long enough. So they leave after their few hours at the gym.

Her other says on the way out, you are beautiful, who wouldn't want to chat you up?

She smiles and says, stop it.

Believe me, I trust you, you're not like my ex. She was a nightmare in every way. Anyway, no need to talk about him now. You're safe and happy that's the main thing.

True she says. Look at you. So handsome.

We're good for each other, touch wood. Want it to stay like this. As they are driving home, she touches the nearest wood that she can find, which is a pencil in the car.

Mutual attraction is what we have.

Three

They usually have a date night.

On date night they meet once every couple of weeks, if they can, to keep the romance alive.

They meet where they had first met and role-play their first date. To keep it exciting and fresh, they book a room at the hotel and make the most of it. The rule is that conversation about work or others is not allowed. No distractions except each other. They make love. Fantasise.

Next day, she leaves alone and so does he. They meet at home.

Back to reality and normality, life goes on. Lots of letters in the letterbox. Here we go again. Bills, bills, bills, they laugh.

Gosh, thank you, he said to her. I can face anything after last night. Okay, not everything, he starts laughing. Not the ex!

They both have children who live with them but take it in turns to see their other parent too.

They treat each other's children like their own.

Gosh, it's getting cold, she mentions. It's okay, you have me to keep you warm.

The heating is on. The house is now cosy. The kids are back tomorrow.

He makes a hot chocolate with marshmallows. Mmm, just what I need.

They enjoy the quietness before tomorrow. Shh, can you hear that? she whispers.

What? Heart beating fast. Nothing.

Exactly.

She taps him on his shoulder and puts her hand on her chest. What do you think? You frightened the life out of me. Tomorrow it's going to be totally different. I miss the kids, don't you?

Yeh me too, to be honest. I thought it was only me.

No, it's not the same without them. They will be back tomorrow.

They sort out the children's bedrooms and lay out their surprises. New pyjamas and matching bedding. Then go to bed.

They each own their own business. She owns a fashion company and he is a photographer. That is how they came to meet in the first place. They were at a business conference. At the same hotel.

Their rooms were next door to each other. By mistake, they were given each other's luggage. They both went down to the lodge to complain. That is how they met. They looked at each other and exchanged their luggage, then went back to their own rooms. They used the lift at the same time, not knowing what to say to each other. Awkward.

Eventually, they had both ended up at the restaurant. She was already there. As they have both discovered already. Haha.

He had been looking at her for a while. It is not as if she never noticed him either. Anyway, he decided to send her over a drink. The bar staff told her that it was a complimentary drink from the gentleman over there. He said, just say sorry for earlier. She smiled and put her glass up to say cheers and thank you.

She calls him over. He walks towards her and replies, you sure? She replies, with a smile, I don't bite. They both laughed and clicked. You know you're beautiful. Sorry, I'm not treading on anyone's toes, am I?

No, it is okay I have been divorced. Single as ever, she said to him.

I am sorry but I cannot accept the drink now. But it was very thoughtful of you. He is into her.

Not being rude, it's just I have a meeting in the morning and have to be on top form.

Next time maybe? he said.

Yes, sure.

Sorry, what meeting is that? You here for the business conference?

Yes. Me too. What a small world.

Okay, definitely after.

She tells him she runs a fashion runway. I have my own styles.

Oh, really?

Yeh.

Amazing! I'm a photographer.

Oh, my gosh. Really good. We have to meet again, even just for business purposes!

As they carried on the conversation they found out that they once attended the same nursery school. The universe had bought them together again. They both felt comfortable around each other. Always a good sign.

We shall meet again, she said when she looked at her phone for the time. Oh, it's ten o'clock. They will not sleep unless I FaceTime them to say good night.

Sorry, who's would they be?

They're my children. Have to go.

He winks at her smiling.

She laughs. Bye.

They exchanged phone numbers. He's happy.

After her call with the children, she phoned her friend, Tina. She told her about who she'd met at the hotel. Telling her that they've exchanged numbers.

He is so hot.

About time you found someone, said her friend.

She replies, yeh, I guess.

Your ex didn't waste time.

The kids are telling me to find someone too. The other day my ex signed me up on a dating site.

Have you been on there to check your matches yet?

I've had a look. No one that I like yet, unfortunately.

Keep looking. Don't lose interest so soon.

Will keep on checking.

You're a catch. Learn to live again girl.

Okay, I will!

As he knew what room she was staying in he calls the reception and asks to be put through to next door, which is her room. Reception asked for her permission if it was okay for them to put the call through from the gentleman from next door. She was quite shocked, and wonders what he wanted? Accepts the call.

First, he apologises for calling her. Then asks if she would want to go to his room for a coffee or a drink. He said, look I'm not trying to get you drunk or anything else, I promise.

Why not, what the heck I need to live a little, I guess.

She goes next door he asks her, what do you want? Tea or coffee?

I will have a glass of wine thanks.

So I still think it's weird how we're in the same place. Wow. Amazing, isn't it? Yeh, most definitely.

They end up giving each other a tight hug.

Gosh did you feel that?

What?

The chemistry between us. Haha, they both laughed.

Yeh, yeh, she replies. I don't usually do this, she said to him.

He replies, what? Talk to a handsome good-looking hunk like me?

Haha. She laughs again.

You're definitely a joker. You have a great personality. I like that.

Oh, so I'm not good looking and he looked at her.

Yeh, you are very self-centred.

Hey if I don't look out for myself, who will?

That's correct.

They picked up their glasses and bumped heads by accident.

Ouch! Rubbing their heads and laughing.

Then their lips touched.

Oh no, sorry.

He replies, it is okay. I'm sorry.

She replies, I kissed you…. Can I just use the en suite?

Yeh, sure, help yourself.

She goes into the bathroom, calls her friend. I've just done the one thing that I shouldn't have.

What's that.

Only just met him and now I'm in his room drinking. Well, one drink.

That's fine just call it a night.

I kissed him.

She looks into the mirror and says to herself, what am I doing?

He calls out. You okay in there.

Yeh, I'm fine, thanks.

She goes back in the room and tells him, I'm going to call it a night. Thanks for the drink and chat. It was nice to speak to you.

See I'm not as scary as you thought. I don't bite. You sure you don't want a coffee?

No, it's fine, thanks.

She went back to her own hotel room and called her friend back.

Her friend asked, do you like him?

Yeh, he's not bad.

Finally, you have hit the jackpot! He is your prize, babe. Haha. Go for it, babe.

No harm in meeting him again then.

That is true, said Tina.

Four

The next day she met him before they went their separate ways. One for the road, I suppose. They had a drink And spoke a little more about each other's interests.

It came on to the subject of children.

Do you have any children? How many children do you have? She quickly established that he had children.

Me too. They do my head in sometimes but it would never be the same without them. They are my world.

Tell me about it, he said.

I still cannot believe we went to the same nursery. Wow.

That we lived in the same city.

He said his parents wanted to move.

What about you?

We stayed in the same place. A lot has changed since then. There is a new complex.

The city has changed. I would be worried if it hadn't changed, he laughed not that I was aware of the circumstances in the first place!

After that, I went to college, uni. Here I am today.

Great. What about you? she asked.

Me? More and less the same really, the only difference is that it was some other uni, for photography. That is where I met my ex, unfortunately. We were over soon as we were married.

Can I ask you something personal?

Yeh, sure, she said. How come you divorced? We just fell out of love. Never really had anything in common anymore. Too many things were against us.

It's weird how you could be so close and in love then, the next minute, break up and unable to live together. I know but it's life.

What can you do?

For a start, we can stop talking about the negative things that life has put us through. Though I wouldn't change having children.

Me neither, he said. I loved her so much too. I guess instead of staying together and arguing in front of the kids it's best to get some headspace and have a break. It is unfair for everyone.

I spent more time at the office than at home. Then when I was at home the phone calls about work never stopped. So much for a better lifestyle!

After their talk, they went their separate ways and back to their own lives.

She spoke to her mom about how she had met him and what a coincidence it was. How they'd got on so well!

Her mom was happy and asked if there was going to be a reunion.

She replies, hopefully, fingers crossed, mom.

It would be good for you. You can't be on your own all your life. I want to see you happy.

Oh, now what have I done, said the daughter.

You okay sweet?

Yeh, it's just that I should have known I was going to get the third degree off you, mom.

They start to laugh.

It is only because I love you and want to see my little girl happy again.

I am happy.

You know what I mean.

Anyway, mom, I think you might have known the mom or the family. There were quite few people that have come and gone. From when you were at nursery.

There was this one woman who I used to see when I used to drop you off and collect you. We became friends as we used to help out at the school. What was the mother's name? she asked.

I think it was Sunita.

Okay. We did keep in touch for a while but as time goes by… Also, remember when I lost my phone and lost all my numbers. That's how it happened. Anyway, see how it goes you never know. It a good family.

Don't wait for him to get in touch with you. He's probably waiting for you to get in touch right now.

A few days went by. She kept thinking of him. Could not get him off her mind. What is happening to me? she questioned herself over and over again.

Reaching out for her phone to send him a message then deleting it instead of sending it. If he was interested he would have contacted me by now, she thought. She checked her emails regularly, she thought he might have sent one. But nope. Oh well, I'm done with waiting. She was disappointed. Oh, well his loss not mine. Never looking back again.

Five

A few weeks went by she receives a message from someone. Totally different number. If it was from a company she would know. Anyway, she answered but as soon as she heard his voice she disconnected the call. He calls again and this time, after a few rings, she decided to answer.

Hey, I am really sorry that I have not been in touch sooner. My phone was stolen.

Yeh, yeh, she said.

I know it looks like an excuse but I'm too busy and I never lie. I cannot do that to you, believe me, babe. I couldn't stop thinking about you. You just pop up into my mind.

She starts laughing. Seriously? Let's meet as friends and take it from there.

Yeh, sure!

Save my number.

He gives her his new email address before saying bye. Then, he called her back and said, sorry, I do apologise, I never asked how you and your family are.

They are all good, thanks.

How very inconsiderate of me. I took my children away. Have to make time for the family!

She was happy and had a big smile on her face when she had finished the call.

Her employee and friend looked at her and said, oooh, look at you. Was that your mystery man?

Yep, he called. He had lost his phone and wallet too.

As long as it wasn't an excuse, it's fine.

We'll be meeting for a drink next week. Not sure what I'm going to wear.

Well, it's not until next week, so plenty of time.

That's true. It's been a while!

She said that it felt as if they knew each other already. Though they had only met once. Well, I suppose they did know each other from the past because they went to nursery together. What a small world!

It's weird, isn't it? Maybe it's time to start dating again. Here I come, watch out world, she laughed.

Later on that evening, once the kids went to bed, she relaxed on the sofa switching from channel to channel over and over again. Glimpsed at her phone here and there looking for a message. She was feeling the urge to send one too. Okay, if I send it, what can really happen? All he can do is say yes or no. I can handle that. Yes, speaking to herself. Gosh, here I go!

Her daughter calls out, mommy, mommy, where are you.

I'm here my sweetheart. You okay?

She goes up to her mommy. I wanted a hug.

Aaah, my sweet, of course, and gives her little girl a hug and a kiss on her cheek. Get some sleep now. See you in the morning.

Mommy, I was scared you were on your own and sad. I want you to be happy like daddy.

I am happy because I have you kids.

No, like daddy is.

Ahh, bless. Okay, don't worry about it now. Let's speak tomorrow after school.

Promise mommy?

I promise, said mom.

Gosh, I had better get a move on. Better get out there and mingle. Even the kids are noticing.

She goes back downstairs to switch off the television and the lamp. There's a message on her phone it says….

Hey, how are you? With a winking smile.

Does this mean we're finally meeting up again? Can't wait don't chicken out.

Erm we will see she sends a kiss emoji. Oh, come on please. You will have to see.

I'm going to call you tomorrow then. Talk tomorrow, babe. Sweet dreams and a few X's after the message.

She goes to bed smiling. By the time she went to sleep it was actually 3 am.

Six

The alarm goes off the next morning. She's happy. Dops the kids to the dad's house. He calls her asking, is everything okay? Are you?

She said, yes why?

It's just the last time you dropped off our little girl she seemed quieter than usual. What about at school too. I've spoken to the teacher, she said the same.

Last night she woke up from her sleep calling me and telling me that she doesn't want me to be on my own anymore. She said her friend told her, her mom is always unhappy. I do not want you to be like that, mom!

You are still in love with me? said the ex husband.

She turns around and says to him, whatever !! You're old news. They both start laughing. You were still coming back to me, remember, she reminded him.

Oh, well.

She will be fine. Probably her age.

No, she said that daddy is with someone and I need to be happy too. At least I know there won't be any tantrums or jealousy, like they were with you, if I did start to date again. Anyway, got to go. Love you, Rita, see you tomorrow.

Can I stay two nights at daddy's, mom?

Of course, baby. Ask your dad just in case he's working.

No. it's my day off. Brilliant. You can stay.

But momm,y you're going to be alone. Don't worry about me. I'm going to be fine. Are you going to see that man, mommy.

What man is that?

No-one, she replies to her ex.

So you have a date then?

No, she must have overheard me speaking to satty last night. She is going through something at the moment.

No mommy, I saw a message on your phone.

Really when? This morning.

You should not be looking at my phone. You know it's wrong.

Sorry. mommy, said Rita.

She hadn't looked at her phone all morning. It said…

I know this is short notice, but are you free today, by chance, for a quick drink? Can't really wait much longer.

She goes to her car quickly and calls him back. Yeh, sure, I would love too! What time and where?

7 o'clock at the restaurant. The one that you said does good food.

That will be nice. See you there, babe.

Do you want me to pick you up?

No, it's okay I will make my own way there.

She looks at the time. Gosh, where has it gone? She puts on her music and takes a bath, singing along to her songs. Then with makeup fixed and hew new outfit on, wow, I do look amazing?

She decided to call her sister, telling her about the date.

Her sister asked, what today?

She replies, today. Yeh, he asked to meet today too.

Oooh, he's keen.

I know.

I didn't even hesitate straight away said yes.

Good on you.

She FaceTimed her and asked, how do I look? Is it too much for a first date?

No, no, you look lovely. You go girl go and get your man. Let me know how you get on. She laughed and said, bye.

Finally, it's time. She looks around for him, sees a man walking towards her. Looks confident she says to herself.

He said, hello, finally, we meet again.

I know, they smile at each other.

Having their meal they got talking and realised they had so much in common.

I'm definitely going to meet you again tomorrow, if you're still okay for that.

Yeh, I'm so happy. Third time lucky!

Seven

They went out for a year. Fell head over heels for each other. Finally, decided to get married and live together.

He also has children. She gets on well with them. In fact, all of the children to get along very well.

Each of them has grown their business.

He is such a romantic. Sends me flowers, never forgets my birthday or our anniversary. I don't like to boast, but yes, I've struck gold this time and don't I know it! she said to her friends.

There is some new guy at the office who thinks he can make a move on me, she tells her friends.

They're all coming out of the woods now, aren't they?

I know. He knows my husband and is his boss too! Haha. He's always trying to make conversation with me. When we all go for our office get-together I will have to introduce everyone to him properly. Definitely. There is a lunch meeting scheduled for Friday. Let's see how it goes.

They had their lunch meeting with some clients and then had to stay overnight. Wouldn't be able to take Rita with them, so she stayed at her dads'.

It went well and they were so great that they could now actually relax and spend some time together.

She decided to go shopping for a few things. She saw a lingerie shop. Gets herself something more sexy and exciting to wear. Got to keep it exciting.

Wow amazing, beautiful colours, especially when they are on you. Though I prefer you without it too.

Haha, she starts smiling.

Come on, babe, don't be shy. They make the most of it, having a great, intimate time together.

She said, every time we do get the opportunity, it feels like when they had first met. So much love, fun and action.

He said, I second that. It's up to us to keep it that way.

They go out for a meal and ordered drinks to their private room. I'm so happy that the deal went well for our next project.

Cheers. This is to us as a great team.

It was nearly school half term for the kids. They would stay with her this time. So, they extended their stay for another day as Rita was staying at her dad's another night anyway.

His stepson, Arjun (but he prefers to be called Arj) was there too. So, they decided to stay a little longer. A little time for their anniversary.

They usually travelled to the hotel where they first met. The hotel that had placed the luggage in the wrong rooms. In each other's room! Role-playing the day they met. Leaving separately. Meeting at the bar and restaurant where they had first met by coincidence.

They laughed when she came down to the bar for a drink and he approached her to offer her a drink. She plays hard to get and declined the offer. He tried again and sends the waitress to say to her could you ask her if she could kindly join me for a meal. She looks at him and he smiles pulling a sad face. The waitress started to laugh because she felt awkward.

She said to her, he is gorgeous. Sorry, I shouldn't have said that.

It's okay, she replies. Tell him yes, for sure I will join him. She smiles.

The waitress goes back and tells him. He raises his arm and said, yes!

The waitress starts laughing he gives her a tip and said, thank you.

They meet and have lunch.

You've still got it in you, she starts to laugh. He gives her a kiss on the lips and they place their food order. They also order one of the best bottles of Champagne for the celebration.

He takes out a ring, an anniversary gift. She was absolutely amazed.

Wow, that is beautiful, my love. He places the ring on her finger.

After the meal, they move to a more comfortable area of the restaurant, where there is a waterfall and the sound of smooth music. Also, a small dance floor.

On the other side, there is also a different bar and a karaoke but no one is brave enough to go up. They stay by the water fountain.

I love this place, he said.

I know, it is so beautiful. It gets better every time.

He places his arms around her while she's sitting on his lap. Touching her face and moving her hair off her face as the wind is blowing a little.

Her arms are around him, he asked, are you cold?

She said, no, but keep your arms around me. That's all I want. I love it when we're so close.

He kisses her and caresses her. I love you.

Love you too, my babes.

Life can only get better. Every time we come here, we have progressed a little more.

They go back to their room.

Let's have an early night tonight.

Yeh, why not.

They both started laughing. As if that is really what is going to happen when it's our last night of freedom. You know that's not going to happen they smile.

She is in the shower. She calls him to give her a hand with scrubbing her back.

No worries, he said. He is happy to help.

Feels good.

He decides to join her in the hot steamy bath.

This is great. You scrub my back and I will scrub yours.

He starts by kissing her, She kisses him back. Spreads the cream all over her back. They enjoyed their steamy time.

In the bedroom, they give each other a massage, then get between the sheets. She wears the sexy lingerie. They caress each other and make love. Let's say no more…

In the morning they make their way back home. On the way, they collected the daughter. She was going on and on about the fun that she'd had.

That's great. I'm glad you had fun. I missed you too my sweet. Bought you and your brother back something.

You okay, she asked.

He said, yeh, just tired.

You can have something to eat with us and then go to bed. Okay, sweet?

Okay, mom.

The stepdad also asked how their weekend went when they told him all about what they did.

We missed you.

The next morning, after breakfast in the kitchen, he dropped the children at school and made his way to work. She is already there. Here we go again. Had a break. It was worth every minute.

The team is doing well and started the process of the new deal for the shows and another side of the business.

Eight

Weeks go by. A few people are off sick. It's December time. It's expected with some people. A few were taking more time out than usual and they were quite concerned about them.

They all kept in touch through WhatsApp. A few were taking over the counter medication and from their GP's. All of a sudden, she had to take over the fort on her own. Her husband had it too. She called it his 'man flu'.

Bless him. He will be back soon. She does not get the 'flu'.

He slept in the spare room so he can get his rest and doesn't spread the germs. Coughing.

She was having to run around. But managed to cope. Twice in the week, they stopped at the dad's.

Unfortunately, no one wants to become a single parent. That is what it was like all over again. Taking sole charge of everyone and everything. Circumstances can leave you in a position of doubt. Or losing someone in other circumstances.

This is very unexpected and unfair, she said to her friend over the phone. As you can only mix with your own little bubble of people. To keep everyone safe. There is no textbook telling you how you are going to feel, she said, I'm keeping the kids occupied making sure they still have some kind of routine. Though it is difficult because sometimes they do not know whether they are coming or going. She starts laughing, bless them.

She replies to her friend, well I suppose I was a single mother for a while before I met him. I trust him I know he will not go astray. He is my boo. If it was the ex, he defiantly would have cheated.

That's why he is an ex and not the one, they both said together and started to laugh.

I do have my support bubble so I guess can't really complain. What about the people who are at this time on their own? I am still lucky.

Sometimes struggles make us who we are today, I guess. There is no shame in asking for help. Especially in hard times.

We have a roof over our head, food to eat. We're all together safe. There is no shame in showing your feelings. It doesn't matter who you are.

That's true, said her friend.

That's why I've made a WhatsApp group with my employees. We need to know they are looked after. Especially the ones who are living alone. Or have young children and have no other form of support.

I am blessed right now. Thank you, God, she said. How did you cope without him really because you are both joined at the hip. She starts laughing.

It's okay. It's not that I haven't heard it before. It was hard but here we are, I guess. Took me back a little.

I made a journal for when things were getting on top of me. I had to be strong for my boo. He was the one that was out there, risking his life just like the key worker doctors and nurses, shop assistants, care worker, waste removers and so on. I could go on and on. Factory workers etc...

Kids grow and have to begin their own lives independently. The sleepless nights. Losing dummies. Staying awake at night looking after them. When feeling unwell. Some amazing days.

Yes, definitely, they laugh.

He recovered. Back to work again. As usual, no matter how careful you are, it is always possible that other members in the household could catch it. As it is airborne. The flu, that is, as it's wintertime.

After work, while the tea was on, everyone was watching television. The news came on about a virus that is spreading around the world killing many people. It is called Covid-19 and it meant that drastic measures had to be taken everywhere to prevent infection from spreading. Some people had to carry on working from home because of being vulnerable. He had to go into the office to keep the business running and keep the money coming in. Also, to help the employees. To provide for their families too.

For her it was that she would not be able to see her husband for a while because he was out there having to mix with other people. She couldn't because she was shielding. So they had to stay away from each other. Not sure for how long, it was unbearable for both of them. They have an en suite and a kitchen on the same floor, so he was able to make food and feel comfortable.

Still in his own house, he was able to relax. Though he too was lonely. They hadn't been away from each other for this long, ever. Heartbreaking.

It was also difficult for the children. He FaceTimes her every day and every night before bed. The kids would also say good night to the dad on FaceTime before bed. He also FaceTimes in the morning before work and throughout the day calls her. Not forgetting the shopping, though most of it was done online. Four weeks went by without any close contact with each other. She would watch him from the window coming back and going to work.

At night they call when they're feeling lonely. Going through a very emotional time is getting a bit much. She is worried about him from the time he leaves the house to the time he gets back home. She calls her work employees and keeps in touch by Zoom, where everyone can keep in touch and support each other. Quite a few have had to work from home.

There was another update and this time it was that all the countries are going into lockdown to stop the infection from spreading. So, everyone was out there doing there last-minute shopping. Stocking up on food, toiletries etc. There was a craze going around for toilet paper. Where people were even fighting for these products!

They would talk about the good times when you did not have to wear a mask and could go to the shops without worrying about whether someone is less than two metres away or not. Also using hand sanitiser every time you touched an item in a shop. Or if you came into close contact to someone at work.

It was getting a bit much for the children too because they too had to do remote learning. Also, we're unable to see the other parents. As co-parenting was going well for the children and adults. There was only so much that was okay.

She was keeping strong for the family, but would go into the bedroom and wanted to scream but decided to start reading to keep the anxiety at bay and by listening to music. She also spoke to the children asking them questions on how they are feeling. Finding something constructive to do. They watch Netflix together.

She was on the phone one night with her husband and he kept coughing. She was worried about him he felt very unwell so he had to isolate and had to have a test for COVID-19. They were waiting for the results. She was saying to him, that's terrible. He received his results in two days and it was negative.

They had to all start working from home as everyone had been told to by the government. So now they were both at home. Eventually reunited. They all had the biggest hug ever. They also cried. The children saw and called it cringe because they all were crying. Then they all laughed and yes, the children were allowed to stay up an extra hour. They all watched a movie on Netflix with snacks and pop. Finally, the kids fell asleep in their beds.

They had some wine and went to their bedroom too. They jumped into bed and couldn't wait to be in each other's arms.

It feels so good, babe. You don't understand how much I've missed you.

I used to have a cry in our bedroom. I could never be away from you either, babe.

The loneliness was so real. I just did not want to speak to anyone really. I was not looking forward to coming home because I was alone. You and the kids felt so far away. Hearing your voices from upstairs was all that was making my day. It was as if my world had come tumbling down, she said.

They hugged. He held her so tight that they didn't want to let go.

They could not sleep all night As they kissed he picked her up and she put her legs around him kissing and hugging him with her hand going through his hair. He pulled the bobble out of her hair which was very wavy and she puts it to the one side and tells him she's covering the light from going to his eyes.

Babe, don't ever leave me again.

Certainly not!

They jump into bed and had a cuddle. Keeping each other warm.

Nine

The next day in the daily announcement there was another change. The schools were scheduled to reopen and although everyone had to keep two meters away from each other, non-essential shops and business, including pubs restaurants, were reopening. So now that meant everyone would be going back to be as normal as possible.

Eventually, lockdown rules were changed, an update on the television.

Thank goodness, they both said looking at each other.

She gets on to WhatsApp to announce that they are going to make a rota. Only a few people at a time will be allowed in the office. The vulnerable employees will have to take the equipment home or have it delivered if they don't have any equipment to improvise with. They also had to make sure that everything was set in place for the employees that were still going to attend the workplace. They had to make sure that the workplace was properly cleaned. Signs in place of two meters on the floor. Hand gel at every desk. Not forgetting the equipment wipes, that will be used before and after using any facilities in and around the workplace.

We have to make it as safe as possible, for all, she said to her husband.

WhatsApp everyone that there will be a meeting on Zoom tomorrow. I'm sure they will all be pleased. For a bit of normal eventually. So, it was time to get into the business mode again! Yay!!

So they started to make a rota of who would be more likely to start at work straight away. As some have to make childcare arrangements. Although they usually have a nursery which is run with the company and solely for the use of company employees. Not everyone is going to be able to afford it right now. Everyone must also have a test done before attending work anyway. For the people who are unable to make their own way, the company is providing transportation home. As long as they can get to work at short notice.

All sorts of things going through both of their minds. He eventually falls asleep. She is still working things out in her head Oh, God, what am I doing?

He turns over in the bed and said, babe, you still awake? Looks at his watch. It's nearly two o'clock. He puts his arm around her to cuddle up with her. Don't worry about anything. We will work everything out in the morning.

He kisses her and says, remember we're in this together. What did we say when we got married? For better for worst, remember.

I know, hun. Sometimes it's hard to switch off, you know.

I know. Only you know how you feel, babe. You're the boss of your own mind, remember. You're the boss.

She eventually falls asleep after listening to some relaxation music of a waterfall on YouTube.

Ten

Next day, up bright and early while the kids were being dropped off at school they organised everything and were ready for the Zoom meeting.

It actually went well, she said, that was a piece of cake.

Next step was to make phone calls for the cleaning. He took over. Called the companies and got people scheduled for the next day. While she made sure that she followed up on some of the clients who had asked for some of her designs. Scheduled meetings on Zoom for the ones that they were unable to make other arrangements for. Also, models had to be booked. Everything was to be with social distancing, so the designs could be seen in person but behind a screen.

It was quite difficult because a lot of people were afraid. Some were getting tested on a daily basis, for everyone's safety. Everyone was ready and happy to do so. Not enough that everyone is now going to have to wear face coverings meaning face masks. This would be throughout the day. It was going to be difficult but essential for now until it is going to be safe not to.

That is when COVID-19 becomes something in the past. Everyone has been told to wash hands regularly and to regularly apply hand sanitiser.

When they set the rota everyone was to do half a day only at the beginning, so everyone gets used to being back at the office. Also, because right now there is not much for them to do but finish the backlog. As there will be no runways at the moment. The makeup was done by the models themselves. As was their hair.

Everything by email. As the shops were closed everything was sold on the websites. All enquiries by phone or emails. Many orders were cancelled.

When they got home, she mentioned to the husband that she at first wanted to become an ophthalmologist who would look after people's eyes. But once she had her degree, she changed direction totally. So, if she wanted to, she could work in an opticians. He was shocked to hear her say that.

But babe, are you sure?

Yes. At least I would be helping. Somewhere. I don't think it's right for me not to.

She decides to apply for a part-time position at her local opticians.

It had been a few weeks and she was sent an email for an interview via Microsoft Teams. She was delighted and over the moon but also anxious because she'd never worked at an opticians.

She was ready. Everything organised and went for it. She was amazed that they welcomed her on the team.

She said to him, oh my gosh, I start next week, babe. Which will hopefully help us. While you run the business.

She went for her first day.

She said, I enjoyed it, but was a bit weird.

He was so proud of her but hardly saw her much until late evening. But they didn't care.

I have so much love for you, babe, like you don't even know.

I know, babe, that makes two of us. You're a bit self-obsessed. They start laughing.

Do you remember when we first met? That's what you had said.

Yeh, I did, they laughed and said, we will do so again. Have our getaway. Once we're allowed to and it's safe.

She comes home washes her hands, has a shower and has a rest with the family. She tells him how only a few people are allowed in at a time. They have to wear personal protection equipment (PPE). That it is quite scary but what can you do.

The job was only for three months because she was only there in place of someone that was off on maternity leave. They were returning the following week. She was shocked that the time flew by that quickly. She was so happy for the experience too. But still had her business.

Gosh, I missed the kids too.

Yeh, when they're over, they've been saying all sorts. Asked if you are safe. When is mom coming home?

But remember the other night how upset he was in the night? Crying, I only want my mom.

I know. It is a shame it can't be easy in their heads. Thinking all sorts. Maybe I'm going to have him in the bed to sleep with me for a day or two. See if he comes out with anything. You can sleep in the spare room.

Spare room, here I come, he laughed. That's me told and kicked out of the room. Okay, boss.

She got up once at night but was okay after that.

I will get in touch with the doctor and see if she can be referred for some counselling.

So, she did that and they referred her to the children's centre from where a phone call was received.

The mother spoke about the way her daughter was feeling.

She will be fine, it's because of the lockdown and feeling of not knowing what is going on, she was told. One minute school is on and the children are allowed to mix with other, the next, a lot of restrictions. It's the same for many adults. Especially the ones who at this time live alone.

Yes, my sister lives alone. There is only so much you can do at home. She leaves the house to walk the dog. Otherwise, she wouldn't go out at all.

At least there will be some support for your daughter and hopefully no more sleepless nights.

She mentioned it to the dad.

She can sleep over? Maybe it will help to have a change of scenery.

The dad is part of the bubble. It is allowed for the children to go there and back. The children were collected by the dad.

Wow, how quiet the house is now. Can even hear a pin drop. They cleaned up, did the necessary checks on the online store that they are up and running. The invoices etc. Made sure everyone had been paid.

Did not realise the time. They realised it was past ten o'clock because the kids called to say good night.

They FaceTimed and all seemed fine.

She decided to speak to the stepmom about what had been going on. To keep an eye out at night for the kids. She was okay and said she had no worries. They have been good having lots of fun. That her son was also there because the dad couldn't have him this week.

So, we have a full house.

Oh, okay. Well, have lots of fun.

We will try. It's a shame we cannot take them anywhere at the moment.

I'm also working from home. It is difficult, isn't it? We will get through. Fingers crossed this COVID-19 disappears soon.

You take care.

You too. Bye for now. Bye.

She gets off the phone and goes to the bathroom.

She shouts out. Babe, I'm going into the bath. I need a long soak after all the strain and stress.

Okay, babe!

She runs the bath, candles lit around the bath. Also, the wave mood light is on in the bathroom. Some music on her mobile phone. Cannot wait to be in there.

Babe, do you want a glass of wine?

No thanks, maybe when I'm done.

Okay. Will be downstairs. Love you.

Love you too.

She managed to have her own little spa day at home. For at least half an hour anyway.

He comes up and asks if she needs her back rubbed.

Yeh, actually come on.

He rubbed her back.

He says, I might as well join you. What do you think? He splashes the water in her face.

Don't you dare splash me in the face.

Oh, what are you going to do about it?

I'm going to…

To what? and they both start laughing.

Splash you back, that's what. She pulls him into the bath. Okay, you wanted to join me, she laughs.

She soaked him. They both laid in the bath.

I was meant to be relaxing. Not anything else.

They get out of the bath in their gowns, not even thinking of drying themselves and jump on the bed.

I can't get enough of you, you know that?

While he strokes her body, she turns around kisses his neck while she is lying there without her gown. They start kissing and make love.

I never want to lose this feeling.

She noticed that he had put rose petals on and around the bed. Petals all the way going down the stairs. When they got down the stairs the table was set, for two. A whole meal and a glass of wine each. With the lights dimmed.

I want our love to keep this way and always to have a good vibe.

Absolutely, babe. You are my soul mate. My one and only. I wish we had met many years ago.

Bad thing to dwell on the past, remember. Although sometimes it cannot be helped.

I know. We have both come a long way in our lives.

They showered and had some hot chocolate with marshmallows and chocolate sprinkles. When the kids were back home, after a few days, they decided to make a time before bed where it would be about how they felt in the day, what they want and what they could change. A feelings group for all four of them.

Each of them was encouraged to speak about whatever was troubling them. The parents only spoke about the children, not their personal lives.

It is great, isn't it?

Yeh, I feel confident and in charge.

It is all about your feelings, babe. If we do not know how you feel we cannot change it.

So then we are all happy. Fair and square.

Yay, the kids said.

Eleven

The next day, after lunch, they had a phone call from her sister. The sister's children were in the background shouting, can I speak, can I speak? So they decided to set up a time for the children to play together, virtually, on FaceTime. They were laughing and joking. Playing all sorts of games.

I am so glad we did this. At least they are not bored and are keeping a relationship with the family. So they keep that connection no matter what.

Yes, we should do this on a regular basis. At least the kids can keep that bond just like they do so with their friends. It's a good idea. So they did that on a regular basis.

Everyone's happy. The therapy was also in place. For both of the children. Everyone is good.

Finally, a celebration.

Hurray!! It's my birthday.

Up bright and early in the morning. I cannot believe where the time has gone. He is 15 today. Everyone has been invited over FaceTime. They will be joining on Zoom when he blows out the candles wishing that his dad could have been there too. But he could not come. Though he had only just come back from his dad's. Well, I've worked really hard on making your cake, hun, especially for you. It has secret ingredients in it.

The boy says, oh no, mom, do I need to get a sick bucket ready? He starts to laugh. Cheeky and smiling.

The music is playing his favourite RnB which he enjoyed but was also a little upset because the family and friends were not all there.

More cake for you, my son. He starts to laugh.

Everything is your favourite.

He enjoyed his birthday and was talking to his friends.

It was a good day after all. Showing off his gifts. It was the very best we could do in lockdown.

When the kids went to bed, she looked on her phone and saw that she had a few text messages from one particular employee. She had been going through a rough time at home but was unable to leave her partner as he had made her feel that no one will ever believe that he is the person she makes out.

Everyone else thinks that he could do no wrong. Other women wish that he was single. He has had so many affairs and recently more because of lockdown. She said life is a nightmare. She has no way of escaping. Everywhere she goes, he goes. So she only manages to send a few messages while he was in the bathroom.

It said, I kept quiet and minded my own business but he keeps mumbling, he can't stand me. That what did he ever see in me. That he has been fucking about. (His words). He said I cannot stand anything you do. That I make him cringe.

Okay, we have to get you back into work. She emailed some phone numbers to her, just in case he tries to lay a finger on her again.

He threw the chair at me.

Right, I'm coming to pick you up. He hasn't hurt you, hun, has he?

No. It missed me. I am not going to allow him to run me out of my home.

Hun, this has been going on for too long. It is a very toxic relationship. Neither of you is happy. Can you not say you're going to your mom's for a few days?

No, because he thinks she will find out about how he really treats me. It is going to look weird, me going there in the week.

Do you feel safe, babe, right now?

I'm going to sleep on the sofa tonight.

Okay, tomorrow we will go to the police station. You have to get out. I will tell one of the others to keep an eye on you too.

No, please, do not tell anyone else just in case the word gets out and he finds out.

Okay, no problem. Your secret is safe with me.

They both look up somewhere for her to live for now.

I know it is not going to happen overnight but we have to do something. You need to feel safe. You shouldn't have to feel this way in your own home. Sorry to say but it's the truth.

She phoned the Samaritans, a confidential helpline. Remember, you do not need to say who you are if you do not want to.

She spoke to someone and they also gave her some information about what to do if she feels that she needs to escape. The number to call or message. (In many languages too). There is always someone on the other end of the line to help and guide anyone that needs it.

I am here for you too. You can come and stay at mine tonight.

He is going to ask where I am going.

He works nights tomorrow. You have the chance to get some things together and leave them at mine or in my office at work, hun.

Thank you. I do not know how to thank you.

Just keep safe, hun. Do not hesitate to ask for help.

She started to get some things together and dropped them at work. There was a message that came through to the boss. That they have a place where she can stay for a few nights in a hostel. She left the house with her things, without looking back.

He went to her workplace asking if she has been to work.

They said, no we have not seen her.

They asked if all is well because he looked angry and he said no, it is okay.

She had reported him to the police a few times before but then decided to say it was okay. Until the last time when neighbours' had reported that there was something going on next door. As if someone was being beaten up and lots of swearing too.

Gosh, poor thing, she said to her husband. I really feel sorry for her.

So, she said to her, what about your place, that is empty isn't it?

Yeh, it is.

Why not rent it out to her?

Well, it is not a bad idea.

So, she moved in and she was worried about the rent but they told her that settle down and as soon as you are able, you can start paying rent. Your safety is what comes first, hun.

They were so happy that she was safe. Her husband, who is now her ex, stopped harassing her once the police had a few words with him.

Every summer they hold a fair to raise money for a charity. Different charities each year. This time they chose to help the victims of domestic abuse. As everyone was unable to get together, they planned activities that people could do in their own gardens and if they did not have a garden, then anything that they could do in their homes like cards, painting, colouring and singing or dancing.

Mentioning that they are doing so for a good cause, it went down very well. All the money raised went to the charity. Which meant a lot more could be done to save more vulnerable people who otherwise would suffer in silence.

It was good to have a break, they both said. A well-deserved break in the house. No holiday.

Oh well, at least we are safe and our families are okay. Who needs a holiday? We have each other!

Twelve

After their break, they went back to work.

They had had a call from a company that loved their fashion and how it was looking online with the effort and effects. There was no makeup artist. The models had to do their own makeup. And no hairstylist. We did what we could. It was difficult but what else could we do?

They loved their designs and placed an order, which was welcomed because it meant more work. Everyone was celebrating with the news. Of course, with tea and coffee. No alcohol allowed at the factory where the clothes were stitched together. They were both grateful to their staff for the hard work and grateful to the models too. At last, we are back on track again.

Soon it was to be Valentine's Day.

Wow! Where has the month gone? It is nearly our special break time. Haha.

She pops out of the office to buy some things for the next week.

She buys herself a sexy outfit. Shows it to someone in the office and she says, Whoo hoo! He's not going to take his eyes off you with that on or is it his hands? they laughed.

Well, that's the whole idea, hun.

The hot tub has got to be cleaned. The lid has been on it so all that needs to be done is for someone to clean it out and fill it up. I will leave that to him. Haha.

Let's hope the weather is better.

Valentine's Day is here. The hot tub is ready and filled. The Champagne and music is prepared. Chocolate covered strawberries. Candles too. Roses in the hot tub. All warm.

The kids looked at it and said, can we get in?

She said, nope, time for bed, hun. It was bedtime anyway.

All sorted. Though a few chocolates disappeared. Haha. Oh well, never mind.

She comes out with her sexy bikini and he also had some sexy trunks.

Wow, you look so sexy, babe.

Come here, she calls him. Oh gosh, can you hear that?

What?

The little girl was calling out. Quick, see if she's okay. Great start. He checked on her she's fine and back in bed.

Then he comes back takes off this gown and jumps in.

Oh, my God, it's so warm in here.

I know, she said, it's amazing.

He pours the Champagne for the both of them. Cheers, babe, happy Valentine's.

You too, hun!

They sip their drinks and place them on the side. She picks up a chocolate strawberry and puts it in his mouth. He does the same to her.

Mmm, they're really sweet.

Not as sweet as you, babe. Aah. Where would I've without you?

It is the best thing we ever did, moving here. How peaceful it is.

Well, that's because the kids are asleep. Hey. Come here. She gets close.

Love what you're wearing or not wearing.

Haha. Yeh, heh.

No seriously babe, you're so hot. When I first set eyes on you, I knew you were meant to be mine.

I know, hun. You too caught my eye too but I had to play hard to get. She winks.

They start to kiss. They have their arms around each other. He picks her up and she places her arms around and rubs her hands through his neck and hair.

I love you so much. Could not be able to live without you, babe.

I'm not going anywhere.

They each put a chocolate strawberry in each other's mouth. He undresses her while she pours some more Champagne. Then they make love. The smooth music in the background.

All of a sudden it starts to rain. Grabbing their gowns, they run in.

Quick, laughing.

Turning everything off and grabbing hold of what they could to take back inside the house.

Trust it to start raining.

We're not going to allow the rain to spoil our night.

They put the fire on in the next room. Cosying up by the fire on the rug. Trying to keep their voices down as they were both having so much fun.

I'm feeling a bit hungry now. She gets her phone and orders some food.

I'm going to have a quick shower, babe.

Sure, have it ready for me after.

The food arrives.

I am so hungry, babe. Built up an appetite.

They enjoyed their food. Finished the Champagne. Made sure everything was safe inside and out on the patio. Went to bed.

It was Sunday.

There were no school uniforms to get ready, as there was no school, so they were able to have a relaxing day. Once the kids were fed and had been collected by the dada and the house was tidy. The hot tub had been cleaned and then had been covered otherwise there would be all sorts in there. For example, spiders!

They stayed in their pyjamas all day. Ordered some more takeaway food, made some hot chocolate then had an early night.

The next day back to work.

The week went by with everything going well. They decided to plan a funday with the children. As it was really cold outdoors, they planned activities indoors. The deal is no one is allowed on their mobile phones. They had bought a 'phone jail' but never used it. So let's use it, guys!

Kids were pulling faces and moaning.

Nope, sorry, it has to be done. We need family time.

So all the mobile phones were placed in the phone jail.

They played many games which involved dancing, exercise and singing. Everyone was having so much fun that there was no need for their mobiles.

We need to try and do this more often.

Yes, babe, you're right.

Time went by and soon it was quite late.

Unbelievable, did not realise the time.

Everyone had fun.

Thirteen

The next morning she got up feeling nauseous. She ran to the bathroom and was feeling sick.

You okay, babe.

Yeh not sure what happened there.

He gave her some water and made her some coffee. Told her to rest and go back to bed.

I will look after the children. It must have been something I ate the last night.

He made some coffee.

She said, oh here it comes again. Please take the coffee away. Seriously, the smell is making me feel worse.

Really! Oh, my God. Do you think you're pregnant? He has a smile on his face.

Okay, let's not think about that, please.

Why not, babe? Best thing to do is get a test.

She wants some toast and tea. Feeling a little better. She carries on not even thinking about it. He came back with a pregnancy test kit.

She took the test and yes, it was positive!

Oh my God, we are going to have a baby. Kids there is going to be another member of the household.

What, really? The boy said, oh no! Not another brat.

One said, I'm only joking.

I want a baby sister, said the little girl.

Nope, I want a brother.

Okay, we will see. Whatever sex it is, we will all love it. They are excited and he kisses her and tells her how much he loves her. The children look at them and say, errrr.

So they start by making an appointment online with the doctor. Then the doctor referred her to a midwife who took care of her throughout the pregnancy up to twenty-four weeks. Then seen by her GP as well as a midwife until her due date.

She was loving chocolate.

Gosh, why am I craving chocolate and also lemons?

She was healthy. Her due date was weeks away. She had to be alone to give birth.

I'm okay with that, she bravely said though she wasn't. She started to cry.

Don't worry, babe, you will soon be out.

I hope so. It took me nine hours last time. Well, I forgot about it after.

They got the room ready for the baby. Let it be a surprise for the kids.

One night she couldn't sleep, tossing and turning.

I cannot sleep either, babe. Every time I fall asleep, you move around and wake me up. I know it is not your fault. She started to get Braxton Hicks, which are labour pains.

They've started, babe. Go and sleep downstairs.

No, I can't leave you like this. I will be okay.

Okay, actually do stay. Look how long it's been since I've had a baby. Why would I put myself through this again? Rubbing her hands over her bump and saying, I'm sorry. I love you. Can't wait to see you.

It's time!

Oh no, shall I call the ambulance? See if my sister can look after the kids so you can drop me off.

Both excited and he is like what is everything in the bag. He checks, yep. All sorted. Extra care is necessary through the pandemic. She had to stay home and protect the baby as much as she can, now and after birth.

She gave birth and came home. Usually, there would have been other family members waiting at home to greet her and the baby. She was not allowed any visitors because of the pandemic. She went home to her family. When she was ready, she FaceTimed and video chatted with the family. Everyone sent their welcome and congratulations cards through the post. Gifts too.

The kids and the dad decorated everywhere. They also welcomed the baby with lots of love. They all had to be extra careful. Make sure that their hands were clean before coming anywhere near the baby. Also using sanitiser on their hands.

It is a happy time for all of us. I am so glad that the birth was so quick. I was afraid of complications because it has been ten years. Wow, life is feeling different!

They made arrangements for someone to be in charge until the baby is a few months. To help around the house.

She said, I'm okay, babe. I can still work from home. So both of them do.

Until a few months at least, babe.

Everyone kept in touch over the phone and FaceTime.

We have everything we need here, don't we, babe.

Definitely, hun.

Love you. Yeh, I know nappy changing duty.

That's the way to be, babe. Take it in turns. Haha.

Cannot wait till your aunts and uncles see you. They are going to spoil you rotten. She was speaking to the baby while feeding her.

The baby making a gurgling sound. Aww, look at her. She kisses the baby on the cheek. Can I pick her up, mom?

Yeh, once she's been winded. Unless you want her to be sick on you.

Er, no. Haha.

Help Is Out There

Support for Sufferers of Panic Attacks
0844 967 4848
www.no.panic.org.uk

OCD Action Line
www.ocdaction.org.uk
Mon-Friday 9.30am to 10pm
0845 390 6232

SANE
Emotional support and guidance for people affected by mental illnesses, carers and their families
0300 304 7000
Daily 4.30 to 10pm

United Against Violence and Abuse
0808 802 0028

National Domestic Abuse Helpline
(Women's Charity)
Freephone national helpline
0808 2000 247

CALM
Campaign Against Living Miserably
FOR MEN aged 15 to 35
Daily 5pm to midnight
www.thecalmzone.net

Men's Help Forum
24/7 stress support for men
By text chat and email
www.menshelpforum.org.uk

Acknowledgements

Thank you to **Specsavers** in Wolverhampton for there amazing support.

And thank you to Richard Millard. It was good doing business with you. Amazing advertising on digital billboards in Birmingham and Coventry.

ADI Outdoor
www.adioutdoor.co.uk

Michael Terence
Publishing

www.mtp.agency

www.facebook.com/mtp.agency

@mtp_agency

Printed in Great Britain
by Amazon

61204368R00047